WAHIDA CLARK PRESENTS INNOVATIVE PUBLISHING

Don't Mess With The Quiet Chick

Niemma's Adventures Uncensored

BD HAMPTON

Wahida Clark Presents Publishing
60 Evergreen Place
Suite 904A
East Orange, New Jersey 07018
1(866) 910-6920
www.wclarkpublishing.com

    Library of Congress Cataloging-In-Publication Data:

Don't Mess with the Quiet Chick
ISBN 978-1-947732-85-8 paperback
978-1-947732-86-5 eBook

LCCN: 2012450975
    1.   Erotica 2. Gay 3. XXX 4. Quarantine 5. White wives
    6. Cheaters 7. Zane 8. Interracial 9. Masks 10 Experimental

Cover design and layout by Nuance Art, LLC
Book design by www.artdiggs.com
Printed in United States

Foreword

Hello, my lovelies! I just wanted to take a moment and thank you for all the support over the longevity of my career that you have given me. I appreciate and love *every single one of you*.

I want you to know that the book you are about to read is unlike anything you have read before. It's a different type of erotica, one that isn't very prevalent in today's books.

COVID messed up many things for a lot of folks, and while everything unfolded, I broke into several new genres: epic fantasy, paranormal fantasy, and hardcore XXX erotica. This novella is meant to do one thing and one thing only— GET YOUR ENGINES REVVED for that SPECIAL night! It is not an urban love story . . . It's not an urban street . . . It's not erotica. And it *definitely* isn't for anyone under the age of 21!!!

It's XXX like you've never seen it done before. It's like a movie but without having to hide anything on your computer. Keep it locked up in your Kindle. It's graphic . . . It's intense. And it's meant to spice up your romantic life.

I hope you enjoy my novella, and after reading this, I totally understand if you are not interested. But if you have been in a relationship for a long time, sometimes . . . a little bedtime story puts your lover *fast asleep*.

Enjoy,
Wahida

Chapter 1

Niiema's Uber pulled to a stop outside of Harlem Nights Ultra Lounge, the best place for soul food in Atlanta. She was meeting her friend Barbie after their last college class of the day. The sun was setting as she watched the orange sky mix in with the incoming storm clouds. Niiema heard a clap of heat thunder and glanced over her shoulder.

Approaching the large bouncer wearing a tight security shirt, Niiema searched for her ID. "Don't worry about that pretty lady, you look old enough," he said with a sly smirk, glancing at her tight white top.

Niiema smirked. She was five feet tall. She had more of an hourglass figure with a perfect caramel complexion, but she felt her legs were her best physical feature, along with her robust booty and washboard abs. She wore her beautiful hair in tight pixie braids with a bright yellow band. Your typical southern bell.

Niiema had forgotten her bra and hoped no one would notice. She thought she could pull it off because she was noticed more for her booty on a normal day, and sure enough, the bouncer had just disproved her theory. His eyes went straight from her ass to her breasts. Just like that, the fact she didn't have a bra on she now knew it was obvious.

Niiema whisked past him when he raised the red velvet rope. She was planning on working out when Barbie called her and asked her to come out for a drink. As Niiema entered the club, she ignored the stares of the wolves standing by the door playing pool. A short man glanced over his pool stick and continued to shoot.

Barbie screamed as she walked in. "Ahhhhhh."

Barbie's yellow skintight strapless dress glittered in the strobe lights. She embraced Niiema in a bear hug. "I can't believe we just closed out the semester." Barbie let her go. "Thanks for coming out on short notice." She glanced at Niiema's hardening nipples. "And I see you're chilly."

"Shut up." Niiema crossed her arms over her chest. She sighed and glanced at the men around the club. "I should have known better and went home to change."

Barbie laughed. "Come on, girl. Let's go get a drink. That will keep you warm or make it so you don't care anymore."

"Oh my God, I hate you!" Niiema said jokingly.

Barbie was a white woman with a light tan and strawberry blonde hair with hot pink tips. She had sky blue eyes, standing only 5'2", a few inches taller than Niiema. She had a nice booty with small perky breasts. But they were both only nineteen, not the legal age to drink. The bouncer from earlier didn't really care as long as he got to fuck one of the college girls at the end of the night. If the management knew, he would have been fired from the classy establishment.

Niiema had never been to the club and she liked the music as soon as she walked in. The latest YoungBoy NBA song blasted through the speakers so loud that she felt the vibrations in her shoes, moving up her legs. Although quiet, shy, and reserved, Niiema could fit in anywhere. A few of the men stared at them as they passed.

Barbie ignored them, but Niiema's gaze fell on a white man standing by the wall with tattoos under his eyes, across his throat, and running down his arms. There was writing on his knuckles, but she couldn't make out what they said. Niiema bumped into a small black stool and her white sneakers stuck to the dried alcohol.

Barbie laughed and glanced over her shoulder at the imposing man leaning against the wall, smoking a cigarette. She nudged Niiema in the ribs. "Go and talk to him."

Niiema gasped. "I can't do that," she said, feeling her heartbeat increase.

"Well, I can." Barbie glanced over again and gave a head nod and wide grin at the man. He caught Barbie's gaze and pushed himself off the wall. Niiema froze, her fingertips scraping the wood of the bar.

Barbie patted her friend on the back and said, "Now be the boss bitch I know you are."

The man approached across the dance floor and smirked. "Hello." Barbie cleared her throat, but Niiema stood motionless, her palms sweating. The man eyed her up and down, his gaze centering on her erect nipples. He grinned. "You cold, darlin'?"

"Nope, not at all!" Niiema snapped.

Barbie chuckled and took a shot. She stepped in front of an embarrassed Niiema and said, "My friend came out on short notice. She didn't expect a handsome fella like you to appear out of nowhere."

"Handsome, huh?" the man said with a chuckle. "That's cool. My name is Derek, but my friends call Big D."

"That a fact?" Barbie asked coyly, her gaze drifting to his belt line. "And why's that?"

D smirked. "I'm six seven."

Barbie glanced up at him. "I thought so." She gave a pout. "That's over a foot and half taller than us."

"Yeah, but if I kneel down we should be almost the same height."

Barbie spit her drink back up.

D smiled devilishly. "Did I say something wrong?"

Barbie grinned. "Not at all, you're saying everything exactly right. Right Niiema?"

"So, you from the ATL?" Niiema asked, trying to change the subject.

D glanced at Niiema, his green eyes making contact with hers. He seemed to be searching her soul for the answer to her question.

Niiema's feet wouldn't move, her knees started to feel weak. She gave a slight nod, tucking her hands under her armpits. Barbie cleared her throat, switching D's attention to her. After a few more agonizing seconds of the music vibrating the air around them, D turned to face Barbie.

"So, since my friend is shy, why don't you and I go out onto the dance floor?" Barbie suggested.

D surprised Barbie by leaning in closer, the smoke exhaling from his nose. He posted his leg up on the stool and Barbie's eyes filtered down to the massive bulge in his tight white-washed blue jeans. Her eyebrows raised.

"I got a better idea. Why don't you and your friend come back to my place," he said, pointing toward the door.

Barbie and Niiema noticed a tattoo on D's hands that read, *Fuck hard.*

That, of course, made Niiema's mind go straight to the gutter and his package. He just so happened to have a massive erection, nearly touching his mid thigh.

Barbie asked," Do you fuck hard?"

D chuckled and glanced at Niiema with a grin. She blushed and very quickly looked down, realizing she had been caught staring. "You're sexy in a shy way, huh?" D said knowingly. "And I got a feeling by looking at those, you wanna head back to the house." He licked his lips at the cloth stretching around Niiema's areolas.

Niiema found herself nodding. Barbie smirked and traced her pink fingernails up his leg to his knee. "I'm game." She stretched her arms wide. "Gotta *blow* some stream off after finals."

D laughed. "Shall we?"

He led them through the dance floor where Niiema's feet stayed glued. She didn't even realize that she had grabbed his hand, spinning him around as Biggie's "Hypnotize" started to play. D lowered his chin and stared into her soft brown eyes. She smiled back up at him as she gyrated her body to the music, her smell teasing his nostrils. Barbie stepped aside feeling the vibe and moved behind Niiema. With one arm, he yanked her back so he was now being sandwiched by both women. Niiema bit her lip as all their bodies intertwined.

Barbie tried to walk away again to let them have a moment of privacy. D's large palm smacked the bottom of her ass cheek. The blow was so unexpected that she paused, unsure what had happened. She felt a hot breath on the nape of her neck.

"Get that hot ass over on this other leg."

Barbie spun around and stepped forward, passionately kissing him. His tongue forced hers back into her mouth as he moved his free hand across her ass cheeks, then slid her over his other knee. The trio grinded to the beat. Niiema felt her lady parts start to warm up as she continued to gyrate. She could feel her juices flowing, attempting to not widen her eyes when his erection rubbed against her melting pot.

D and Barbie stopped kissing. He then turned to Niiema and sucked on her bottom lip. All he could think about was how soft and supple her lips were. She groaned as he flicked her lips open with his tongue. Niiema felt his erection grow even larger. Barbie leaned in and planted her red lips on his neck. D grabbed both of them by their lower backs and pressed down as he stood up.

Barbie groaned loudly as she felt the cloth press against her naked parts. Niiema's tight black workout pants started to become increasingly wetter as her arousal heightened. D lifted both their heads back and hissed. "Let's continue this at the house." He nipped at Niiema's neck. "I'm gonna show you why you should never be a church mouse."

Chapter 2

Exiting the club, a young valet brought a two-door silver Mercedes with onyx handles up to the curb. Barbie and Niiema glanced at each other as D tipped the man, who opened the passenger side door. Niiema lingered by the curb. "There doesn't seem to be enough room."

D smiled. "Y'all two can sit together for a bit. My place isn't far from here."

Barbie nodded. "I'll take the bottom," she said, sliding into the red leather seat.

D stared at Niiema. "C'mon, beautiful. You can sit on your friend's lap. It won't be long," he glanced at his dick, "before you're too busy to care."

Niiema walked over to the passenger side and climbed onto Barbie's lap. She felt extremely self conscious from the warmth her mound was letting off. Barbie gasped when she sat down. She leaned into Niiema's ear and whispered, "I see someone's excited."

Niiema blushed.

D sat down and reached across to the glove box. He pulled out two joints and placed both to his lips, sparking them to life. He handed them one and he smoked the other. "Y'all ready?" he asked as he accelerated.

Niiema had never smoked weed and if her parents ever found out, they would kill her. She was raised in a strict household where drugs and alcohol were forbidden, as was premarital sex. She often preferred a quiet day at the library, or singing the Lord's praises on Sundays, than a night out. She had, of course, slept with the boys in high school like every other teen. But drugs and large dicks were totally foreign to her. She figured she had to become cultured, it was the rule, not the exception.

Barbie tapped Niiema on the shoulder and held the joint up to her lips. "It's okay, let the steam off."

Niiema just stared at it. She wanted to smoke the joint, but she didn't really know what to do. D sensed her trepidation. As they came to a stoplight, he leaned toward her and gently touched her chin. He parted her lips and blew the smoke into her lungs. She coughed violently and Barbie rubbed her back.

"You good sis?" Barbie asked.

Niiema glared at her friend and said, "What the fuck?"

"That's chronic, it's that good shit. My bad, I should have told you not to inhale so much," D said before chuckling and kissing her.

She kissed him back without hesitation. Barbie caressed her shoulders. Niiema froze like a deer in headlights when D slowly slid his hand over her breast and teased her nipple.

Both of them instantly hardened under his rough fingertips, causing them to forget they were sitting at a traffic light. Horns sounded behind them, as the light was now green. D slammed the gas pedal to the floor, causing Niiema to bang into Barbie's chest and drop the joint.

"Damn," Niiema muttered as she searched for it.

Barbie squirmed out of the way and in the confusion, Niiema grabbed what she thought was the joint. She heard Barbie gasp, but she didn't move. "Uh, Niiema, that's not the joint."

Niiema blushed, realizing she was just caressing Barbie's soft spot and quickly withdrew her hand. "Oh my God. I'm so sorry."

D twirled both joints in between his fingers. "Ladies, I have the joints."

Niiema's head was swimming after the first shotgun hit. She rubbed her fingers on her black pants and leaned her head back against Barbie's shoulder with a sigh. Barbie smirked and pushed her pixie braids out of her face.

"I'm so horny," Niiema mumbled, touching her breast. "It's been a long while."

D glanced over and slid his hand up her thigh, making eye contact with Barbie. "You should help your friend," he whispered while switching lanes.

He handed Barbie the joint and caressed Niiema's breast, his knuckles pinching her nipple. Barbie held the joint up to her lips and pressed it against them. "Take another toke sweety, it'll feel great, I promise," she said as she placed wet kisses on the nape of Niiema's neck, blowing hot air on the trail she left.

Niiema groaned and took a deep pull. This time she exhaled quickly and didn't cough. She shifted her weight, rubbing up on Barbie once again. Barbie let out a delightful gasp. Niiema got the vibe that Barbie was more than enjoying herself from the heat radiating off her womanhood. A moan escaped Niiema when she parted her lips to take a long pull off the joint D lifted to her lips.

Barbie's sky blue eyes caught D's and she leaned forward and gave him a shotgun, the rest expelling from her nostrils. They stared at each other for a long time. Barbie licked her lips as she and D eyed Niiema's exposed neck.

D mouthed to Barbie, "Go for it."

Barbie took another long toke from the joint. She had been attracted to Niiema since meeting her the previous semester. But neither of them had ever talked about sex with other women. Barbie had slept with many women and with D's encouragement, she let go of her inhibitions toward her friend. She parted her lips, planting kisses on the side of Niiema's neck, while sliding her hand up her shirt and rubbing on her breast, circling her areola as she grazed her nipple now and again. D was rubbing and touching on Niiema's other breast.

"We're coming to our stop," D said, pinching the joint between his lips.

"Finally!" Barbie moaned.

Niiema slid D's hand back to her breast as he pulled up to the curb of his brownstone on Peachtree. He moved his hand to the door handle and shut the car down. Niiema glanced over at D as Barbie began to lick circles around her neck. Niiema groaned and arched her neck, the hairs on her back tingling.

"D, please touch me some more before we go in," Niiema said, quieter than she had ever been.

D smiled and rolled the window down. "Whatever you say, church mouse." He tossed the joints into the street and slid closer to them. Barbie started sucking on Niiema's neck as D gently lifted her white shirt, ensuring the rough cotton fabric touched her nipples as it was raised. He slid a tattooed hand up and gently pressed it, then slid his head over and started sucking it.

Niiema groaned as his other hand slid to the outside of her soaking wet black pants. He pressed his palm to the top of her mound and pressed his index finger into the cloth. Niiema squealed. Barbie started sucking her neck harder. Niiema managed to slip one of her hands under her leg and inch it to Barbie's wet spot.

Barbie grunted and ground against it, Niiema's fingertips stopping a few inches away. She could feel the heat pulsating from it. Barbie continued sucking Niiema's neck. D leaned back and watched, rubbing his erection. After another few minutes of kissing sounds and fingers nearing crevices, he leaned forward. "You two ready for a night you'll never forget?"

Chapter 3

D opened his car door, closed it, and then walked around the back of the Mercedes. Both women were panting and grinding when he opened the door. D smirked and stared down at them from above. He lit a cigarette and enjoyed the show in the cool breeze. After another few minutes, he lightly tapped the window.

"Ladies." They turned to him. "If y'all don't mind, we can go to the house to finish this."

He helped Niiema out of the car first and then made eye contact with Barbie, who slid one leg out, letting him get a glimpse under her dress. She licked her lips, staring at D's dick, and slid the rest of the way out. Barbie brushed past him and slid her finger along his massive cock, sashaying arm in arm with Niiema.

They stopped at the stoop as D slid past. He unlocked the door and opened it. Niiema leaned against Barbie with a giggle and licked her lips as she passed him. D watched them walk by, his eyes glued to their asses. They ensured he watched the bottom of their cheeks press against the fabric as they stood in front of the steps leading upstairs.

"Where to?" Barbie asked, sliding her finger up Niiema's leg while she flicked her ear with her tongue.

"Second floor. It's the door on the right," D said, leaning into Barbie's ear.

They took the first step and then D slapped them both on the ass. They both turned. "Hey, that hurt," Niiema said.

"Is that a fact?" D asked, slapping the other cheek, sending a jolt through her lower back.

She bit her bottom lip as D spun her around and gently pushed her forward. "Now, we can continue."

Both women made eye contact. Barbie giggled, and they took the steps up to the second floor. They could hear D light another joint as they ascended the steps. Reaching the top floor, they stopped and D reached around them and unlocked the door, while sliding his other hand between Niiema's legs. She parted them and gasped as he tapped on the edge of her womanhood. He threw open the door and then swept both of them inside to the foyer.

The apartment was massive. The walls were painted in a soft yellow and next to the foyer was a large kitchen with marbled floors and custom made cabinets. "Don't take your shoes off," D said, walking into the kitchen.

Niiema was sliding her shoe off when he said it. She slipped it back on and glanced at Barbie, who was quickly pushing her breasts up. She teased her nipples and then braided her hair in pigtails. "What are you doing?" Niiema asked.

"Preparing to get my head yanked back," she said with a giggle. "I hate when men yank on my neck. If I give them handlebars, they take to it like a fish to water, honey." She glanced at Niiema's pixies. "Has anyone ever snatched you by the braids?"

Niiema lowered her chin and shook her head no, her self confidence receding once again. Barbie smiled into the mirror. She handed Niiema a rubber band from her purse. "Tighten it in a bun so he just grabs your shoulders."

"And if I want him to yank my braids?" she asked with a smile turning up the corners of her lips.

Barbie gave a curt laugh. "Your head will hurt like hell in the morning. Trust me, tie 'em up."

Niiema snickered and adjusted her braids into a ponytail. "Sorry about earlier, I have never smoked weed before. I didn----"

Barbie turned and kissed Niiema passionately. They searched each other's tongues for several moments and then Barbie leaned her forehead against Niiema's. "No, it wasn't an issue." She ran her fingers along her arm. "I've always been attracted to you, but you're really prim and proper, and I was scared you might think I was weird."

Niiema smiled and chewed on her bottom lip. "I'm glad you did. I wanted to kiss you too."

D leaned against the door frame with a bottle of champagne and three glasses. He reached over to a dimmer on the wall closest to him and turned the lights down low. "I see y'all two are getting acquainted past friendship."

They both smirked and Barbie ran her fingers along Niiema's shoulder, then kissed it softly with a purr. "I'm glad she came out tonight."

"So am I," Niiema said, clenching her knees together to stop her wetness from soaking through her pants.

"Follow me," D said, leading them into the living room.

Niiema and Barbie held hands and walked behind him where a joint, hooka, and long green bong were on the table. There were remnants of coke on a mirror, but D slid that away from them as they sat down. Barbie's face lit up when she saw it.

"I forgot to ask what you do," Niiema said, sitting close to Barbie.

D scoffed. "I'm a drug dealer." He smirked. "I can't afford this on the salary of a working stiff."

"Ohhhhhhh," Niiema said, noticing some of the drugs were stacked neatly in a corner across from them.

D shrugged. "I was a basketball player in college a few years back. But I got in some trouble. I ended up homeless and then I got back on my feet." He nodded at the drugs in the corner, then shrugged. "Didn't really grow up wanting to go this route." He cleared his throat. "Not exactly romantic talk, is it?"

Niiema reddened, knowing she had killed the mood. Barbie came to her rescue, sliding in front of her. "Can I hit that bong?"

D shrugged. "Be my guest. But it ain't just weed in there. It's laced with ecstasy."

Barbie smirked and leaned forward. "Never tried that. Here goes nothing. Niie----"

Before Barbie could stop her, Niiema slid forward, snatched it off the table before she could, then threw her lips around it while she stared D in the eye. She fired it off. The smoke barreled down the shaft and into her lungs. She withdrew and coughed so hard she felt like her lungs would explode.

Barbie rubbed her back as she coughed and gasped. She spat on the table and grabbed her temples as the hit spun her head in a million different directions. D watched her wither and cough, and a few moments later, she gave one final cough, then sat back on the couch, her eyes wide open.

"What the fuck was that, Niiema?" Barbie shouted.

D just smirked. "So, the mouse isn't as quiet and shy as she seems."

Niiema laid her head back and gave a groan as the weed took effect. Barbie stared at her in shock and awe. She had never known Niiema to ever try a cigarette, let alone a hard drug. She glanced at D, who was filling her glass with a dark liquid.

"Get this down her, she'll even out," he said.

"No way, I don't even know what that is," Barbie said, staring at the glass.

"It's whiskey. She'll feel better. Either your friend is crazy or insane to take a massive hit like that to the head her first time. I'm not gonna drug you, that's not my bag. If it were, I wouldn't have brought you to my place."

Barbie took it and gave it a sniff. She took a tiny sip to test it, then gave it Niiema, who sat up with a sway.

"Ah, a good and loyal friend is hard to come by," D said.

Niiema took a small sip at first, then another. "I fucked up the mood again, didn't I?" she mumbled.

D stood and stretched, his erection pressing through his jeans. "No, not all. I like aggressive thinkers, though I imagine your drug use days are over. Which is fine." He lifted Barbie by the hand. "Let's allow her to shake that off."

Barbie glanced at Niiema. "I'm fine. Continue with the party," Niiema said.

"Okay, I'll just be in the other room," Barbie said.

D took his shirt off. "Nah, no need. We'll save that for tomorrow." He yanked the bottom of Barbie's dress over her head in one motion. She gasped as she stood in front of him in only a bra, the tan lines from her bikini showing. "You like that don't you?" he asked, taking her chin in his fingers before kissing her on the lips.

Barbie was aroused more than she had ever been. Her mound wetted. She glanced at Niiema again, who winked and licked her lips before she slid her hand to her wet spot. Barbie was up for the challenge. She shoved D with everything she had and he fell back on the couch. He tried to get up, but Barbie tugged at his belt, her knees straddling his thighs. "I wanna see this monster."

D grinned and grabbed her by the ass, lifting her over his head. She gave a yelp as he planted her over his lips. "Me first," he said, slamming his tongue into her.

Barbie moaned and held her palms to the wall. D took her clit in his mouth and sucked as hard as he could, sending a wave of pleasure through her. She licked her lips and tilted her head back, rubbing one of her creamy breasts. D held her close and shoved her whole pussy into his nose and mouth. His long tongue slid near her ass and back into her, over and over.

Barbie let out a loud gasp as her toes curled. "Holy fuck," she screamed.

She spared a glance over her shoulder and watched

Niiema sliding out of her leggings and spreading her legs wide. They stared at each other as D ate her out, Barbie nibbling her pink fingernail. Niiema slammed her fingers inside of her as she gazed at D's bulging muscles. Barbie turned back around and gripped D's head. She bucked and the corner of her mouth curled as she came; something she was very self conscious about.

She shuddered for a few moments, and then tilted her head back letting out a loud scream. D stood from the couch while keeping her in his mouth. Gripping her by the waist, he continued sucking, slurping, and spitting. He gazed into Niiema's eyes as he did. Barbie's ass cheeks were at his throat and her head rested between his knees. She shook again and then whimpered as he slid his index finger over her clit, flicking it.

"Oh my fucking G-----" Another orgasm hit her, constricting her stomach muscles. Her head lifted and she held on as long as she could before screaming his name. "Deeeeeee."

He lowered her softly to the couch and eased her back onto the pillow. Her eyes were barely open as she held her wet opening. She had never cum that hard in her life. It felt like wave upon wave of the ocean had crashed against her clit.

"You alright?" D asked, sliding her blond hair strands behind her ear.

"What the fuck was that?" Barbie heaved, trying to catch her breath.

D laughed. "I call it the clit-a-whirl."

"It's a clita something," Barbie moaned.

D handed her a glass of champagne. "I'll go see to the

mouse over here." When he reached Niiema, he leaned over and touched her chin softly. "You okay, Mouse?"

Niiema nodded. "I'm good. You ate her out like a mad man."

"Your turn, Mouse." D gently slid his arms under hers and kissed from her breasts, across her stomach, and then lifted her higher around his shoulders.

"Good luck on the clit-a-whirl, Niiema," Barbie teased.

"Clit-a----"

She didn't even finish as he held her above his head and slowly flicked her clit. She moaned and gripped his ears. He slowly lowered her onto his face and began to slide his tongue on her clit. She shuddered and gasped. "What the f-- ---"

D slammed her down on his face until her knees shook and then flew wide open. She gently let go of his ears and felt light as a feather. He massaged her booty as he continued to suck. He rolled his tongue around her clit, feeling it harden. Then he took it between his teeth and continued to pull at it. She screamed and glanced at Barbie, who rubbed herself while she watched.

Barbie slowly rose from the couch, got on her hands and knees, and crawled seductively over to them with her ass high in the air.

She tugged at D's pant leg and pushed his knees open until he stood shoulder width apart. "Here comes the clit-a-whirl," Barbie cooed from below.

D slid his hands up Niiema's back and gripped it tight, then lowered her down so she was even with Barbie as he continued to suck. Niiema's back arched and Barbie held her head. "Wait for it," she hissed into her ear as D slid his lips over her clit and slammed his tongue inside.

Niiema shook so hard her head slammed side to side. "Oh my fu-----" She trembled and shook again, the ecstasy taking effect. She tried to pull away as her pussy pulsated, sending wave after wave of orgasms through her body. Barbie comforted her, licking her earlobe, and tugging on her dark nipples lightly.

"It's okay, Niiema. Just let him take you over," she whispered in her ear as she sucked on her earlobe again.

Niiema screamed and gasped for air until her abs contorted like Barbie's had. She attempted to pull away again as Barbie hurried to unbuckle his belt, her eyes focused on his massive bulge. She managed to free the belt as Niiema flung her arms back, blocking her access.

"Keep cumming," Barbie encouraged her, pinching her hard nipples.

Niiema lifted as her stomach screamed at her for a break. She finally gasped with a long hiss and went limp in his arms. D lowered her to Barbie, who cradled her as she took Niiema in her arms. Tears ran down Niiema's cheeks as Barbie held her tight. The emotional barrier had been released, all the pent up frustration bursting forth.

"Did that really just happen," she let out breathlessly.

"Yes, sweety, it did." She glanced at D's cock. "But something tells me that was only a minor bit of what we will experience tonight."

Niiema rolled onto the floor, exhausted. "I'm not sure if I can continue," she gasped. "This has never happened to me."

D knelt beside her and cradled her head. "C'mon now, Mouse. You can handle it. You hit the bong like an expert. Now…" He rose to his feet and glanced at Barbie. "Help Niiema up while I get you some water. This next part is gonna blow your mind."

Niiema's head lolled side to side as Barbie cradled her head in her lap. She managed to turn over and kiss Barbie on her stomach. Barbie glanced down.

"I want to taste you," Niiema said, glancing out from under long eyelashes, her mascara starting to run from her tears.

"Are you sure you have the energy?" Barbie asked, eyeing her warily.

Niiema sighed and sat up. "I'll get my energy back. The ecstasy is making me cum a hundred times harder than usual."

D walked back into the room with a couple bottles of water, a bottle of lube, and some ice. He took a seat on the couch. "I think I'll watch for a few minutes."

Niiema pushed her braids out of her face and laid Barbie back against the front of the couch. She tepidly inched her face toward Barbie's wet spot and slowly touched the tip of her tongue to her clit. Niiema had never been with another girl.

Barbie shut her eyes, her mind at ease. She peeked one eye open and watched as Niiema's mouth descended on her clit. She bit her pinky nail and moaned. Niiema took to giving head like a fish to water. She heard Barbie whimper and watched her bite her lip.

"Now, Mouse, do I need to show you how it's done?" D

asked from behind them, stroking his shaft.

Niiema shook her head with a loud slurp and then wrapped her arms around Barbie's booty and slid her forward on the carpet. Barbie moved with her and waited. Niiema glanced over at D. "I'll show you how it's done."

"That's the style, Mouse."

Niiema stuck her tongue out, turned the tip up, and spread Barbie's pussy with two fingers. She jammed her tongue inside till no more would fit. Barbie's legs slammed shut. Niiema gripped both her knees and slid them back open. Niiema took Barbie's trembling hands and placed them down on her head. She pushed them down and Barbie slammed her pelvis up as Niiema wedged her tongue deeper.

Barbie gripped Niiema's head, screamed, and threw her head back. She bucked as Niiema drove her tongue as far up as she could. Using one hand to press down on her pelvis, she directed it to an upward angle. "That's it, Mouse. Give it to her," she heard D's voice encouraging from behind her.

Barbie shook uncontrollably and gripped Niiema's braids tighter. Niiema kept her pressure up and pressed her mouth down as hard as she could before swallowing her clit. Barbie arched her back and then felt D's iron like grip on her throat. Her eyes snapped open.

"Anyone ever done this to you?" D asked.

Barbie reached up his leg in response while she gasped and slid her hand over him. "Harder," she muttered, unsure exactly who she said it to.

Either way, they both went harder. D leaned forward and snatched one of her pigtails and slid her open mouth closer to his massive erection while loosening and tightening the grip around her throat. Barbie gasped and then pushed Niiema from her position. Niiema went to protest until she saw D choking Barbie.

She paused, unsure what to do. Barbie gasped, "I'm okay sweety, it's making me hornier."

Niiema smiled and lit a joint from the table nearby. She took a deep pull and held it. She slowly exhaled, then took another long drag. "Oh, Mouse is a pro now?" D said with a smirk.

Niiema crawled over slowly. D stared at her apple shape ass, licking his lips. She moved to the other side of D's jeans and slid her hand over Barbie's, who's eyes were rolling back in her head. D released Barbie's throat and she gasped, rubbing her clit furiously. He leaned forward and slapped her gently on the cheek. "Okay, Barbie. Now, it's your turn."

Barbie slid across the carpet and kissed Niiema, flicking her black nipples as D unzipped his fly slowly. Both women were rubbing each others parts, lost in the moment.

"You ladies ready?"

Barbie and Niiema broke apart and both licked their lips with grins on their faces. He slowly reached in his boxers and rubbed himself for a moment. D started to withdraw it, but before he could, Barbie asked, "Can we take it out?"

D grinned. "Be my guest."

Both of them slid their hands seductively up his thighs then crossed over to where it was tight against his pant leg. Barbie purred, licked his jeans, and slid one hand up to his black and red boxers while Niiema did the same.

"Ready?" Niiema asked.

Barbie gave a furious nod, her pigtails flopping.

They slowly lowered his boxers while staring into his eyes. They both reached it at the same time and gasped. When the boxers slid down his thick shaft, their eyes opened wide. His massive white cock skyrocketed out in front of them. They both snickered. His shaft was perfect. With two inches of girth and nearly eleven inches long.

"Can I go first?" Niiema hissed while she pressed two fingers against her clit with a moan.

All Barbie could do was nod, her eyes glued to it.

Niiema attempted to wrap one palm around it, but her tiny hands only covered half of it. "Use two hands, it works better," D whispered from above.

Tentatively, Niiema moved her other hand from her dripping wet spot and closed her fingers together. Barbie watched as she flicked the tip of her tongue over the opening, tasting the salty precum. Barbie leaned in and flicked her tongue over it and licked her lips.

"My mouth won't fit around it," Niiema said with a little defeat in her voice.

"No one's ever does, Mouse. Just suck the head. I'll marry the girl who can."

Niiema opened her mouth wide and managed to get the tip of the head of his dick in her mouth. She gave a long pull until her mouth started hurting. She stretched her jaw out and tried again, this time fitting the whole head in her mouth. She pulled back and glanced up. "I want to try something."

"Oh?" D said with a chuckle.

"I want Barbie to shove it down my throat with your help."

D laughed. "You think that'll work, Mouse?"

"Worth a try."

Barbie leaned in closer. "You sure, Niiema?"

Niiema nodded.

Barbie leaned in closer and whispered, "Have you ever done this before? I know you girl. You're a church girl."

Niiema scowled. "I'm not miss priss."

She opened wide. Barbie sighed and slowly slid her fingers through Niiema's braids. Undoing the rubber band, she gently pushed her neck forward. Niiema gagged and withdrew. "Shove it down, Barbie, please. I want to feel it touch my tonsils," she pleaded.

"Okay. But if you choke to death on his cock, I'll never forgive myself."

D chuckled.

Niiema opened her mouth as wide as she could and took the head. Barbie pushed both hands against it and shoved. Niiema's whole body shook with a gag and her knee lifted up. She reached behind her and slapped Barbie's ass. Barbie smirked and pushed harder.

Niiema burped and gagged again, then withdrew. "Now you help, D," she said, spit dripping from her chin.

"Mouse, this ain't Everest. You don't have to die trying."

Niiema snatched his balls and yanked with a scowl. D grimaced. "Okay, Mouse. It's your call."

Niiema opened her mouth wide and Barbie shoved her head back down. She gagged again and D placed his hands over Barbie's, interlocked them, and gave a light push. Niiema choked again and wiggled her mouth side to side, inching it further down her throat. D gave a low groan and felt the tip hit her tonsils. She dry heaved and shook.

She slapped Barbie's ass again, and Barbie pushed harder. D heard her suffocating and tried to pull out. Niiema grabbed his ass and pushed forward. Her choking grew louder until she managed to take six inches in all. Her whole body convulsed, and they let go. Niiema fell back with a loud gasp and coughed. Barbie hurried over to her.

"You okay?"

Niiema spat, the spit dribbling down her chest, and inhaled again. "Yup. But nowhere near finished. I'm…close…to…the…top of Everest" She jumped to her feet and shoved D onto the couch. He glanced up with a look of awe on his face. "Now, shove it down my throat for real this time. Barbie, rub your pussy on his face. He met his match tonight."

Barbie was in shock as she kneeled, watching Niiema dart between D's legs and slam his dick down her throat. "Fuck her face," Barbie giggled.

D grabbed her by the braids, a bunch in each hand, and shoved it down her throat until her legs kicked back. He let go and she spat on the shaft. She kept it up until nearly eight inches had been swallowed. D couldn't believe a tiny woman like Niiema could get further than any woman had ever gone. His knees grew weak and his cock pulsated.

He moaned loudly. "What the f----"

Niiema came up for air and snatched Barbie by the pigtails and kissed her. Barbie licked the spit from her chin and crawled over to D. "Your turn."

Niiema slid behind her as she took D's cock in her mouth. Niiema's brazenness must have sparked something inside of Barbie, who was well versed in sucking dick because she grabbed D's hands and shoved them down on her blonde scalp. She gagged and continued. She slid her palm to his balls and pulled them as far out as they could go.

D groaned and Niiema gripped his throat. "Now, get ready for our dic-ta-whirl."

She hopped off D and helped Barbie as she gagged. Niiema whispered in her ear, "Go get him," she hissed, pushing D's legs up.

He gave her a quizzical look and then it dawned on him. He backed up and held his knees high while Barbie tugged on his balls. Niiema slid under Barbie as she gagged and worked his shaft, only managing to get four inches.

"You gonna stand there like a pussy, or are you gonna handle your business?" Niiema asked before slapping him across the face.

D licked his lips. "Oh, it's like that, Mouse?"

Niiema spat on her fingers and rubbed his asshole. He took one giant palm and slammed her head under his cheeks. He hissed as Niiema massaged his inner thighs. She pulled back, inhaled, and started again.

"Holy fuck, you two are gonna kill me!"

"Stand up," Niiema demanded.

D raised an eyebrow. "Oh, the mouse has fangs?"

D smirked and stood as Barbie's chokes intensified. She yanked his ass forward as Niiema parted his cheeks from behind. He gave a loud groan as Niiema buried her face in his crack. D didn't know what to do. He'd been with more than two women at once, many times over. But tonight was different. He had met his match, and the night would only get spicier.

Chapter 4

D glanced over his shoulder but Niiema's small frame disappeared. He felt her tongue licking his asshole and a shiver went up his spine as she flicked his balls from behind. He staggered, accidently driving his dick further into Barbie's mouth, who pulled back with a deep gulp. He mouthed sorry as Niiema continued to lick him.

"I think you have him on the ropes," Barbie giggled, as she pulled his dick out of her mouth. "He almost pushed that monster into my stomach."

Niiema made kissing sounds between his ass cheeks, which made D even hotter. "What the fu-----"

Barbie cut his sentence short as she hopped onto the couch, evening their height difference, and started choking him, her nails digging into the side of his neck. He cut his eyes at her and saw the lust emanating from them. He attempted to move, but he saw her look of determination as she tightened her grip until he started choking.

He gave an animalistic growl and choked Barbie back with one hand, pressing Niiema's head further into his crevice. Barbie threw her head back and moaned with a gasp every few seconds. Then the unthinkable happened.

Niiema wheezed as she pulled away. She stood up, walked to the table, hit the bong, and picked up the bottle of lube. She remembered a porno movie she had once stolen from her brother when they were younger. Niiema popped the top open and smeared the jelly around her middle finger.

D was too busy choking Barbie and vice versa, each choking in a testament of alpha dominance. Niiema knelt back down with a grin and parted one of his ass cheeks. She licked it and then slowly slid her finger along the crevice. While Barbie and D battled one another to see who would last the longest without air, Niiema did something that never crossed her mind with the few partners she had.

Blame it on the ecstasy.

She licked his hole once more and then slid her fingernail into his ass. D gasped as Barbie released and stiffened. "What the fuck?" he muttered.

Barbie glanced behind him and laughed. "Take it like a man, D. Let her have some fun. I've never seen her like this."

"I knew I shouldn't have given her any E, she's fucking cra----"

Niiema slid her finger up to the first knuckle as D gasped. The plan ended there. She had no idea what to do after she did that. Barbie sucked D's bottom lip as he stiffened even more. "I'm gonna go show her how a pro does it. Hold your knees if you can't take it. Have you ever had this done?"

"Had what done?" D hissed, unsure whether he should

run away.

"Been milked," Barbie said with a giggle.

D shook his head. "Oh, a fresh case. Let me make sure you get the full ride of a dic-ta-whirl."

She hopped off the couch as D groaned and leaned over. Barbie knelt beside Niiema, who was frozen in her tracks. "What now?" she hissed.

Barbie smiled and traced her fingers along Niiema's shoulder, then up her neck. She kissed her, Barbie's tongue swimming in her mouth. Niiema smiled when their lips parted. "Let me show you how to do this right the first time."

Barbie grabbed the bottle of lube, rubbed it across two fingers, and winked. "This is called milking the prostate. He's about to have the biggest orgasm of his life."

Niiema chuckled. "I'm not even sure why I thought of this," she whispered.

Barbie smirked. "Girl, just grab a joint and watch how experienced girls preform."

Niiema reached for it on the table and caught D's eye. He wasn't mad, she could see by his light blue eyes. He wasn't happy. He was horny. He winked at her.

"Oi, Mouse. You sure you're a church girl?"

Niiema held the joint up to D's lips and lit it. He took a long pull. "I thought you were the nice one."

"This is only the beginning," she cooed, returning to where Barbie was lubing her fingers.

"So, this is a pretty simple way to intensify his orgasm so he cums so hard his knees will go weak. Spread his ass cheeks," Barbie instructed.

Niiema knelt behind Barbie and pressed her palms

against his white skin and pushed them apart.

"D, this is gonna feel weird at first, then you're going to feel like a coke high a few minutes later."

D nodded with a grunt. "Alright, but if you hurt me, I'm fucking you up."

"Idle threats, D," Barbie said in a sing song voice.

She inserted both fingers at the same time like Niiema had. She heard D gasp and tighten up. "Relax, D."

His ass cheeks relaxed. Barbie gave a coy smile to Niiema. "So, you insert your two fingers and aim them forward. You're looking for a walnut sized gland called the prostate. Once you find it, you roll it in circles, and when you hear the guy gasp, you press down slowly at first until you feel his breathing increase, then as he cums, you press down *hard*."

Niiema nodded. "How hard?"

"Really hard," she said with a wink.

"So, what do I do?"

"Put his dick in your mouth, silly."

Niiema shrugged and crawled around to D's front. She picked up his massive cock and held it in front of her. She glanced up at D and batted her eyelashes. "Are you ready to cum, Big D?"

D nodded, his eyes half open. Niiema rubbed his thighs. After she heard him gasp again, she took him in her mouth and started sucking the head, rubbing her erect nipples as she did, all the while staring up into D's eyes.

"Oh my God," he shrieked.

Niiema planted both palms on his groin and started driving his cock down her throat. D grabbed her braids and rolled them over his palm. He proceeded to push more of his girth down her wet throat. He gave several more deep breaths as Niiema watched Barbie slide her fingers in and out. D sat perfectly still for a long moment as his breathing increased.

"This has never happened," he shouted, showing the first signs of emotion.

Niiema kept bobbing, the slurping sounds driving Barbie faster. "Pull his balls when I tell you," Barbie said.

Niiema nodded and placed her palm around them. D winced, then took a deep haggard sigh. Feeling like he was about to orgasm, Niiema yanked his scrotum down with everything she could. A few seconds later with loud gasps emanating from his throat, he tapped Niiema's held lightly. It was supposed to be the sign to pull off, but Niiema went harder and faster. D gave a loud moan and then with a shake of his hips, Barbie pressed down hard on his prostate. He ejaculated so intensely that he screamed and launched his head back, his eyes rolling back with them.

Barbie kept the pressure up and Niiema gagged from all the semen shooting down her throat. She gagged as she leaned back and held on, using both hands as he continued, swallowing what she had received. His knees shook and his toes curled as Barbie kept applying pressure. D's lips turned into a sneer. His back arched as Barbie finished milking him dry while Niiema stared at her.

D dropped to a knee as Barbie slid under him, licking his balls. Niiema kept jerking him until his tip was red. She gave it one last peck and lay back. D landed next to her, his breath coming in gasps. Barbie snuggled into Niiema's arms and rested her head on her breasts.

After a minute of trying to catch his breath, D glanced in

their direction. "Well, there's a first time for everything. But I'm gonna get you two tomorrow after breakfast, believe that," he said, passing out.

Chapter 5

The first rays of sun burst through the partially opened blinds. Niiema's eyelids fluttered and then opened. Barbie sat on the couch smoking a blunt, still naked. Her pigtails were a mess and she could only wonder what she looked like herself. She sat up and glanced around.

"Where's D?" she asked, her voice raspy.

"I'm in the kitchen making breakfast. Get yourself a shower, I'm taking y'all shopping," he shouted.

Barbie smirked. "We aren't escorts, D."

"Nah, not like that. I'm not taking you to Prada. I'm taking the mouse somewhere she's never been."

"Never been?" Niiema asked, taking the blunt from Barbie's hand and taking a toke.

"You'll see," D said with a smile through the opening in between the kitchen wall and the living room. Niiema felt her sticky chin. "Hey D, mind if I take a shower?"

"Make yourself at home," D said, pointing toward the back.

Niiema picked up her workout clothes and glanced at Barbie and whispered, "I have no panties or a bra. What the hell am I supposed to do now?"

Barbie pointed at some bags over by the wall. "D ran out first thing this morning and got us some stuff to change into. Your bag is blue, mine is pink."

"How'd he know my size?"

Barbie shrugged. "I told him while he ate me out this morning."

"Ugh… you got head on the couch while I was asleep? That's nasty."

"No, we went in the bedroom. You have been asleep most of the morning. We've been up for about four hours now. I caught another clit-a-whirl to start my day."

"What time is it?" Niiema asked with a chuckle.

"About one in the afternoon. Go shower up, I already did. I just felt like air drying my lady parts after last night."

Niiema laughed. "Okay, I'll be right back."

She walked to the blue bag. D's eyes were searching her hour glass curves intently while licking his lips. Niiema smiled and picked up the bag. "Thanks, D. I appreciate you doing this."

D walked in with a plate of pancakes. "No problem at all. Made breakfast if you're hungry."

"Not yet, but I'll eat later."

D smirked. "Suit yourself, Mouse."

"That's my new nickname?"

D shrugged. "Meh, better fitting for a church mouse to be called Mouse."

Niiema laughed and walked into the bathroom. The inside was larger than it appeared. There was a double sink with a tube of toothpaste and a bottle of Listerine next to one. And travel packs of toothpaste, tooth brushes, and soap at the other one.

Niiema found a pre-rolled pink towel smelling of lavender that was so soft it glided across her fingers. She walked to the porcelain tub and ran the water. She noticed water jets surrounding the inside and a new loofah hanging from the drain. She stepped in and tested the water. It felt refreshing.

She slowly sank into the bath and when the water hit her clit, she remembered the night before. She had never had so many orgasms in her life in one night. Most of the boys in high school came and she never felt a thing, other than them groping like wild boars rooting through a briar patch. All sniffing and eating with no real course of action.

She took the loofah and lathered it with soap. She washed herself and as she approached her spot, she hesitated. Her clit felt like it had been rubbed raw, which it probably had. She snuck the sponge under the water and waited for the pain. None came.

She dabbed at first, ensuring she wouldn't wince. After a few tender strokes, she washed herself clean, making sure she wiped her face at least half a dozen times. With everything washed, she hopped out of the tub, drained the water, and fluffed her braids out. She tied them in a ponytail and opened the bag.

Inside was an exquisite strapless red silk dress. She held it up to herself and stood in front of the mirror. She placed it beside her and found a pair of black lace panties and a matching bra. She put the underwear on and then pulled the red dress over her head. Unopened mascara and lipstick were sitting next to the toothbrush and Listerine.

She flicked her eyelashes with the wand and brushed her teeth. She gargled with the antiseptic, spat, and then glided her red lipstick over her lips. She puckered, checked her teeth, and walked back to the living room. D and Barbie were talking in hushed tones and when she approached, they changed the subject.

Niiema sat down and picked up a few grapes from a platter nearby. She popped them in her mouth. "So, what y'all talking about?"

"We were discussing how much E makes you hornier and crazier than a three legged dwarf, riding a three legged mule in a china shop. No one has *ever* taken that much of my meat. Been fucking a long time and that was a first for me on many fronts. I hope I can repay that pretty soon," D said, lighting a blunt.

"Oh, I thought you were prepared to get bitten by a mouse."

D laughed. "Yeah, I was, but you have a special ability."

Niiema wrinkled her nose at him. She glanced at Barbie's outfit that seemed to be the same quality as her own. And knowing her like she did, Niiema knew she wasn't wearing any underwear. Barbie crossed her legs under the table and tapped Niiema's.

"You ready to go out and see where D is taking us?" Barbie asked.

"Sure. Classes are over."

They rose from the table and D carried everything into

the kitchen. "What's with this guy?" Niiema asked.

"What the hell do you care? He's hot, has a huge cock, and is nice. What more can you ask for?" Barbie said, pulling her shoes on.

"For him not to be hot, have a big dick or be nice. I wasn't preparing to spend the weekend getting clit-a-….whatever he calls them. I have to get to my parents' house this afternoon," Niiema replied, shoving her feet in her shoes.

"No one's forcing you to be here, Niiema. You can go if you want. I'll get my pussy sucked on till the day I die. I love that clit-a-whirl. There is nothing better."

"Except the dic-ta-whirl you created," Niiema said with a smirk.

"I'm not the one who grabbed the lube when I was high off E. I had to save you from running your uncoordinated fist up his ass."

Niiema grinned. "That shit makes you horny as hell."

"Try coke one time and you'll see how it really is on a clit-a-whirl," Barbie said, moaning.

"Not doing that," Niiema said as D walked into the foyer.

"Not doing what, Mouse?"

"Um, nothing. Let's go see this shopping place and then we'll decide what to do from that point on," Niiema said, opening the door to the hallway. She walked down the hall and took the stairs faster than she intended to.

The trio walked out of the house and over to the Mercedes. "We won't be taking that one, ladies. It's my everyday driver."

"Everyday driver?" Niiema asked.

D shrugged and started jogging across the street. "I'll be

right back," he said over his shoulder.

A few minutes later, D pulled up to the curb in a bright canary yellow 2020 Ferrari F8 Tributo. The car looked like it had been driven out of the Grand Theft Auto Series. Niiema and Barbie stared at it, both calculating the cost of the vehicle.

He popped out and opened the passenger door. "Ladies."

They smiled at each other. Barbie slid in first and Niiema hopped on her lap. "You got anymore E?" Niiema asked quietly.

D shook his head. "I don't think you'll be needing that anymore. It just brought out your wild side a little faster than you would have shown it before."

"What wild side?" Niiema asked, sticking a braid behind her ear.

Barbie laughed. "Do you not remember last night?"

"Kinda...I know I woke up and my pussy felt like it had been kicked last night."

Barbie snickered. "Yea, by a giant tongue."

D smirked. "And you...."

"What?" Niiema asked, her skin flushing.

She had been fully aware of her actions, but her E hangover had blurred the images. She remembered the clit-a-whirl, but she had orgasmed so many times she couldn't remember what act made her feel what.

D hesitated. "You...." He sighed with a chuckle. "*Y'all* milked my prostate."

Then it dawned on Niiema. She remembered starting but not finishing. Barbie whispered in her ear. "You took his load. I did the finger banging."

Niiema cleared her throat. "Oh."

D laughed. "Hardest nut I ever had, and I've been with a lot of women. Hell, I was in porn a few years back too. Nothing like that happened in the movies I was in." Niiema and Barbie laughed with him.

As they flew down the street, Niiema watched the buildings zip by. The city skyline appeared around them and they switched to an off ramp, heading into the city. D drove past the gawkers and pulled up in front of a large warehouse with tinted windows. Niiema gave a look to Barbie, who shrugged. "We're here."

"We're where?" Niiema asked.

"You'll see," he said, opening his door and sliding out.

He walked around the trunk, adjusted his growing erection, and opened their door. He extended his hand to Niiema, who joined him on the sidewalk, then Barbie.

"Don't you have a car with a backseat?" Barbie asked, smoothing her dress out.

D shook his head. "Nope, I mostly fly solo. If one has no friends, then one can't be betrayed."

Niiema swallowed the lump in her throat. "Kinda a shitty way to live," she said before walking to the door with him.

"In my business, it's the only way to live and get up the next day. You get used to it after a while." Niiema nodded. "Y'all ready?" he asked.

Both of them glanced at the door wearily.

D smirked. "There's no danger here. Only pleasure," he said, pulling both doors open.

Niiema and Barbie stood in the doorway and stared into the shop. Half of it was a weed dispensary and the other half was a sex toy shop. Barbie nudged past Niiema with a grin and stood a few feet away. She inhaled and sighed.

"Wow, that smells great. I want to live in here."

D's fingers brushed against Niiema's. He winked and walked in behind Barbie. Niiema followed them in, her eyes glued to the floor. As much as she wanted to be there, she felt guilty because her parents would have killed her had they even suspected she was in a head shop with sex toys of every shape and size, along with dildos in various colors, as well as large and small vibrators. The list was all inclusive as her eyes searched the area.

Barbie wasted no time and walked to the counter. "An ounce of chronic, please."

"That'll be forty-seven fifty," the clerk said.

Barbie felt her side, forgetting she had left her wallet at D's place. She turned to D. "I forgot my wallet."

The clerk glanced up. "Whaddya say, boss?"

D glanced at both Niiema and Barbie's faces and said, "My guests are on the house today. Get whatever you want. But no hard stuff from the back, just a few ounces of weed."

Niiema's eyes was still searching the shelves. "I don't think I need any weed, but there's some cute lingerie over there."

"Okay, get as many pieces as you want." D turned back to speak to the clerk. "So, how's business today, Stevie?"

"It's steady. Everyone's been coming here this morning to get your latest product," he said, handing Barbie her sealed baggy.

Barbie raised an eyebrow. "New product?"

D chuckled. "Yeah, that bag is the hardest hitting chronic

from this dispensary."

"Aren't dispensaries illegal?"

"Sure, if the cops find out, but to them we're just a sex toy shop." He grinned. "What they don't know, they don't need to know."

D glanced over at Niiema, who was holding the lingerie up to her chest. He licked his lips and Barbie caught him. "You like her, huh?"

He cut his eyes at her and Barbie laughed. "D, it's okay." She touched his arm. "She likes you too."

"I don't do relationships."

"Who said you had to?" She smiled. "She is a very quiet chick. No one ever goes after them. But if they did, they'd find the wildest pussycat on the block."

She walked away and left D to his thoughts. She stepped beside Niiema and kissed her on the cheek. "So, what goodies are we getting?"

"I'm not sure. I like all the lingerie, but I've never used a vibrator or a dildo." She cast her eyes down. "Never really been like this before."

Barbie giggled and nudged her. "Buck up, girl. Tonight will be a night we never forget." She held a tight see-through piece of lingerie up to her chest and clucked her tongue. "Yep, this will do for a few minutes before he rips it off." She glanced over her shoulder. "He'll be inside you tonight, Mouse. You might wanna stack up on some supplies. I doubt a dick that big would even fit in a rubber though."

Niiema rolled her eyes. "You really gonna call me Mouse now?"

"What?" Barbie shrugged her shoulders. "It fits. You're

quiet as a mouse, but when the cat's away, you play. Not everything has to be so black and white…well, no pun intended. But if you continue to live your life like an aging nun, that wild pussy and mouth you got will dry up and wither away like a sand dune."

"You're impossible."

"Yeah, and you're a church girl finding herself. I'm not impossible, I just say what you're thinking." Barbie glanced around and stared down an aisle. "Let's find some toys for tonight. I haven't had a dick in my ass for a long while."

"You're disgusting," Niiema spat.

Barbie gave a coy smile and said, "Okay. I take it you've never taken a dick in the ass."

Niiema gasped and slapped her arm. "Absolutely not. And I never would."

Barbie chuckled. "We'll see about that."

Niiema stormed off to the dressing room as D came up. "What was that all about?"

"Oh, just girl stuff. She's never been in a situation like this. I know y'all like each other." D went to interrupt, but Barbie raised her hand. "Look, I know you do and it's all good." She glanced at his package. "I'm just saying that she is fragile, and I know you see her a certain way. Just make sure you know why and don't *fuck her hard* like some kid in junior high school."

She stepped closer and stared up at him, the lust blazing a hole in his eye sockets. She thumped her finger into his chest and said, "But you *better* fuck me like a whore. I'm no prissy quiet church chick." She grabbed his testicles and yanked. "I'm a boss bitch and I'll cut your sack off if you don't put my head through a wall. Get me?"

D just stared at her. No woman had ever talked to him the way she had. He had to admit, it made his dick hard, but he knew that he liked Niiema and wouldn't dog her friend out in front of her and treat her like a cum dumpster. He leaned down so he was nose to nose with her. "If you want that kinda fuck… you'll get it, but you're not gonna thump my chest like you some real boss. I'm the fucking boss, you hear me, bitch?"

Barbie grinned. "That's better, Daddy. I want that dick in my stomach. Now, when can I get that?"

"You take care of Niiema and I'll meet you in my office. Ask her to get us lunch and pick you up something." He glanced around and then viciously slapped her across the face.

Barbie snapped her head back and grinned. "I'm gonna fuck the shit out of you, Daddy, so you can make love to your perfect quiet girl tonight while I watch."

D glared at her. "If I do this, you fuck off after tonight and leave her in my hands. Deal?"

"So, you do like her, huh?"

"And what of it?" he spat.

Barbie licked the blood from her lip that she got from the slap. "I just know." She moaned and rubbed her breast. "I'll do whatever you say, Daddy. I just want to get it like I love it, and I know you won't do that tonight." She pouted. "Unless I need to beg for it."

"Nah, I'll take care of your slutty ass so she doesn't feel uncomfortable tonight when we do our group thing. I know your type."

"Oh, funny you should mention that about my ass." She brushed her breast against him as she snatched a tube of lube from the shelf. "I'll be in your office shortly."

Niiema walked over to them. "Hey y'all, I found one I like."

"Hey girl," Barbie said as she approached, sliding her hands over her lip in a fake yawn.

"D has some business stuff to deal with and I offered to organize some shelves. He needs something at the house. Can you get it for him?" Barbie asked, crossing her legs to prevent her wetness from sliding down.

"Sure. What does he need?" Niiema asked, glancing at him.

D stuttered. "Ummm, I need my briefcase that I left near the front door. Would you mind if Stevie gave you a lift back? I'm not sure you can handle the Ferrari just yet."

"Oh yea, anything I can do to help. I really appreciate you hanging out or whatever that was last night," Niiema said with a shy smile.

D cleared his throat, his heart skipping a beat. "Thanks, Mouse." He whistled to Stevie. "Oi, Stevie, give Niiema a ride back to my pad." He tossed him his keys. "I got some business that came up."

Stevie nodded. "Sure boss. You good with running the joint by yourself?"

"I did it before you started working here, kid."

"You got it boss. We'll be right back."

"Sounds good, man. Thanks." Niiema walked away to follow him. "Hey Niiema." She turned and he bent down and kissed her softly on his lips. "Thanks."

Niiema blushed and bit her lip. "No problem. You good, Barbie?"

"Oh, I'm great. I will help *any way* I can, too."

"I'll see y'all later," Niiema said, following Stevie out the door.

After Niiema left, Barbie said, "Alright, motherfucker. Enough childish shit. You better bring the smoke or I will follow you two around until I get what I want," she snarled, and slapped him across the face.

Chapter 6

D stared at Barbie, his eyes narrowing, a cold dead look in his eyes. "Bitch…." He felt his lips. "Did you just fuckin' smack me?"

Barbie stared up at him. "Fuck yeah I did you pussy. I'm not timid little Niiema."

D snatched her by her hair with a growl. He dragged her across the floor, kicked the rubber, swinging the door in, and flung her in the office. Barbie spat on his shirt and licked her lips, her desires to be completely dominated being fulfilled. It had been too long.

He yanked her head up and went nose to nose with her. "You wanna get dominated?"

Barbie spat on his shirt again. "Those letters on your knuckles better be a true statement."

D snatched her by the neck. She gasped as he dangled her two feet off the ground, staring her straight in the eye.

"Okay, slut. I'll let you know why they call me Big D." He dropped her. She gasped for air and held her throat with a grin on her face. She squealed as he spun her around with one hand, his other gripping her blonde hair in a death grip. She gave a loud groan and twerked.

He wound up with one hand and smacked her as hard as he could across the ass. She screamed out. "Smack me harder, Daddy."

D slapped her ass cheek again with as much force as the other and slammed her over the desk. "This is gonna be a quick job because I want to wash your slut smell off me before she comes back."

"Then fucking do it, you piece of shit."

"What was that?" he asked, lifting her dress up, revealing her naked ass.

"You heard me." She slammed the bottle of lube on the counter. "Stick that motherfucker up my ass and don't stop until it bursts from my throat."

D hated to admit it but Barbie's complete and utter slutty behavior drove him wild. He loved slutty women; they were the only kind he dealt with. Niiema was a new idea. He pushed the thoughts from his mind. "Put this motherfucker in your mouth and shut the fuck up." He shoved her to her knees.

Barbie reached into his jeans. "Yes, Daddy."

He unbuttoned them and his cock roared to life, bursting from his boxers. "That's what the fuck I'm talking about," she shouted and gripped it with two hands.

She shoved the tip down her throat and D snatched her neck. "You ready for the Big D, bitch? It's gonna knock your tonsils out," he shouted at her, gripping her throat and hair.

Barbie rolled her eyes with a sigh and slapped his bare ass. D showed no mercy as he hammered her throat. The gagging, the spitting, and the wheezing all happened so fast. Tears streamed down her face as she gagged over and over again.

He withdrew as she gasped for air. He leaned down. "You alright?"

She slapped him across the face. "Don't be a bitch."

"Okay, now it's on, whore."

He snatched her head again and slammed so much of his shaft down her throat that he had to pinch her nose shut. She gagged, her feet kicking out behind her. She dry heaved over and over as more spit dripped from her lips. He withdrew again. "You had enough yet, Barbie?"

She spat on his shaft. "For the moment. Now, fuck me in the ass," she shouted, throwing her skirt over her ass as she spun around.

D snatched the lube off the desk and popped the lid. He squirted a giant glob in his palm and lathered his dick. "Didn't know you were such a freak," he hissed as he slapped her ass with his shaft.

"This ain't nothing," she said with a loud scream, slamming four fingers in her pussy from under her legs.

D watched her fingers slam her hole. A slight smirk crossed his face. "You ever take an eleven inch dick in the ass? It could really hurt you."

She huffed loudly. "I AIN'T Niiema for fucks sake. There's a first for everything. I can't be this dirty around her, so let me have my moment and you two lovebirds can sing your song tomorrow and I'll be out your hair. Now, sling that meat motherfucker, and make me squirt."

D grinned. "I'll show you who's boss."

He rubbed a dab of lube on her asshole and held his palm over her fingers as they swished her juices around. She screamed and her eyes crossed as he slammed down on it, creating a barrier over it. "Do you have a dildo or vibrator around here. I want to feel like I'm being DP'd," she moaned.

D reached over behind the desk with his long muscular arms and yanked out a rabbit and a large black dildo. "Will these do?" he hissed in her ear.

"Sure will. You got any coke? I really want to have a really loud, mind blowing orgasm."

D shook his head and lifted a wooden box lid near them. "Be my guest" he said, rubbing his cock on her milky white ass.

Barbie grunted as he pressed his pelvis against her ass, driving her fingers almost to the last knuckle. She tapped some coke out of the baggy and chopped up a rail. She lowered her face to the desk and took it like a hoover vacuum. She rubbed some onto her fingers and held it behind her for D. She gave a loud groan as the drug blew her serotonin levels sky high.

D lowered his nose instantly and took a nostril full. The coke blew through his veins, widened his eyes, and hardened his dick as his head reared back. He yanked Barbie's soaking wet hand away and handed her the dildo. She slammed it up to the hilt with a loud scream. Her eyes crossed, which they always did when she was having sex while high.

D snatched her hair and yanked it back. She slammed the dildo all the way in and screeched. D shook his head, slammed her head down next to the coke, and lined his cock up.

"Move my head a little closer, I want to sniff when you fuck my ass." D held the coke in his hand and held it under her nose.

"Fuck me," she shouted as she snorted every ounce off his palm then licked it. D started slowly. No matter how much some women wanted rough violent carnalistic sex, it was still eleven inches and two inches wide. To just ram it home with no care about hurting someone wasn't his modus operandi, ever.

Barbie slowly slid her hands to her ass cheeks and parted them while she choked on the coke. She kept snorting more with deep loud moans and grunted as his tip neared it. She spread her legs wide and put her chin on the table. The coke was smeared across her lips and nose, her eyes glazed.

D slowly slid the tip in and Barbie gasped, then gave a loud sigh. She brought one hand back around and mopped up the rest of the coke, rubbing it on her gums. D inched in, her asshole widening. She screamed and snatched the vibrator and brought it to her clit. She pressed it against her mound, and it started humming. D poured more lube over his shaft and inched in a little more. Barbie slammed both palms on the desk.

"Now, slam that motherfucker in," she shouted, glancing over her shoulder.

D grabbed one of her shoulders and slowly slid it in. After four inches were in and the lube began to work, Barbie let out an explosive scream. "Ohhhhh fuuu----" She withdrew the dildo and squirted. Her body convulsed from both the orgasm, the coke, and fucking her friend's crush. The act sent her into overdrive as she rubbed her palm over her opening.

"That's it slut. Big D got something for ya," he shouted, pressing his hand over hers, burying the vibrator deep within the folds of her wet spot.

"Keep going D, I can…I….."

Sweat dripped from D's brows as he shoved another three inches in. As he slid further in, Barbie screeched and bucked, her whole body convulsing. Another squirt followed, causing her to buck harder and faster. She rode up his shaft more than he pushed. After another minute of her cumming constantly, she had taken nine inches in all.

D stared in disbelief. She glanced over her shoulder, bit her bottom lips and moaned. "Daddy, go balls deep. I'm ready for it."

She furiously rubbed her clit with the vibrator, dragging it back and forth. D gave a groan and pressed both palms over hers. "Here comes the Big D," he groaned, and jammed the remaining two inches in.

He couldn't believe that she had taken the whole thing. She screamed so loud that he thought someone would call the cops. He snatched her breasts and cupped them in his hands as her body shook, her eyes crossed, and she gasped in ragged breaths.

"I'm gonna cum aggggg-----"

She slammed up and down on the desk, D's balls slapping her ass cheeks. She screamed, slamming her fists onto the coke stained desktop as the orgasms ripped through her body. D gripped her hips and began to slide out. Barbie collapsed on the desk. After a moment, she threw him a towel lying nearby. "Wipe it off and fuck my pussy before she comes back."

"I thought you wanted it in the ass."

"I did and now I want it in my pussy…." She purred, touching her breasts. "And I want it balls deep in there, too," she moaned, and ran one hand through her hair. "Come on, Big D…. give me that motherfucker balls deep."

She laid back on the desk and propped her knees up. She gave him a coy finger wave and he strode over to her, wiped his cock off, and snatched her by the hair. He slammed into her so hard that she squealed. "I've taken plenty of big dicks in this hole. Ram this pretty white pussy."

D slammed his palms down and pressed his weight down, locking her knees on the desk. Her bare wet pussy was scorching hot. She groaned and bit his neck with a purr. D slammed his dick in without waiting for her to accept him. She clutched his shoulders as they made eye contact. He could feel her hot breath on his cheek as he pounded away to her screams.

"Daddy, fuck me harder," she shouted, sucking his earlobe. "Bang it till I can't walk."

D grunted and kept slamming. Barbie's legs slammed against the desk. "I wanna feel it deep." She kept hissing in his ear. "Give me that nut."

D lowered his chin and found his rhythm, fucking her as hard as he could. He felt the pressure mounting, then something happened that he never experienced. Barbie gave him a cold smile. "I told you I want this nut."

Her walls clamped around his shaft in a death grip. He

couldn't pull out as hard as he tried. "Hey, what the fuck? Let go of me, you crazy bitch," he shouted, pushing her legs away.

But it was too late, the coke had numbed his senses and he ejaculated with a loud roar. He shook as she milked him dry. His hot seed shot deep into her. He gasped and blinked his eyes. She finally let him go and he stepped back. "Tell me your crazy ass is on the pill," he demanded.

Barbie rolled her eyes. "Of course I am, silly," she huffed. "I'm not crazy."

D gave a sigh of relief. "I don't make it a habit of nuttin' in a woman I've known for a night."

Barbie climbed down off the desk and lowered her dress, smoothing it out. She tossed her hair and fluffed it out. She smiled and patted his cheek, then kissed the other one. "Trust me sweety, I don't want your kid either."

Chapter 7

Niiema walked back into the store and watched as D and Barbie walked out of the back. D was tightening his belt. Her skin flushed when she figured out why she got sent away. Barbie smirked as she approached. Niiema thrust D's briefcase into his chest and stormed out.

D sighed and shook his head. "Fuck," he muttered.

He chased out after Niiema. "Hey, slow down a sec, will ya?"

Niiema kept walking until D gently touched her wrist and turned her around. "What D?"

"Why are you walking away?"

"I may be shy but I'm *not* fucking stupid. You sent me away so you could fuck Barbie without me in the room," she spat.

"Mouse, I won't lie. You're right."

Niiema glared at him. "I'm right? You're not even going to lie?"

D shook his head. "Look…" He took a deep breath. "Last night was the first time we met, and I didn't expect to start liking you."

Niiema crossed her arms over her chest. "It was sex, D. That's all it was."

D bristled. "Maybe to you, but I wanna get out of this game. The drugs, the whores, all the bullshit."

"D," Niiema said exasperated. "You know nothing about me."

D smiled. "I was hoping to change that."

Niiema glanced around his shoulder and spotted Barbie twirling her blonde hair by the door. "Bitch," she muttered under her breath.

D rubbed his mouth. "Fuck."

Barbie strolled over. "Niiema, there's a reason why I asked you to leave," she said.

"Yeah, so you could fuck him without me. I know there's no set rules, but I wanna feel good too and you two just sent me away like I'm just some simple girl who fell off an apple truck and landed in the big city." She paused. "But I'm not."

Barbie gave a nod. "I know, sweety, but D won't be vulgar around you because he likes you, which is fine. I just love having sex a certain way."

Niiema's iris' shrunk as she stared through her. "And how would you know what I like or don't like?"

"You said anal was dirty and you would never do it. I've always fucked big dicks. I love when I get anal. It gives me a very hard orgasm. I knew he liked you and he didn't want to make you uncomfortable." She rolled her eyes. "Which is what it is."

"So, you sent me away so you could get what you wanted

and thought I wouldn't find out?"

D got defensive. "Mouse, it's not like that. I told her that if I gave her what she wanted, she would just let it be you and me."

"Why?" Niiema shouted.

Barbie snickered. "He just wants it to be y'all and for me to fuck off. No skin off my nose, but for me to leave, I had to take it in the ass." She groaned. "Which was awesome. I told you a cok----"

D stepped in front Barbie to prevent her revealing the rest of the story. "Mouse, I'm sorry. If you want me to drop you off at your folks house, I can do that."

Niiema lowered her chin, fighting back tears of anger.

Barbie tapped her fingertips. "Niiema, I'm sorry too. I didn't mean to be so shellfish, but I didn't expect you to go into overdrive last night. I think it's best if I just leave."

Barbie turned to walk away. Niiema snatched her by the hand as she turned and pulled her close. "It's okay, I kinda get it. You've been protective of me since we met. Do you like him?"

Barbie laughed and eyed D up and down. "Only thing I like on that boy is his cock. You know my usual type," she giggled.

"Yeah … tall, dark, and handsome," they both said at the same time.

Niiema smiled at her. "Let's go have some fun together. If it works out between me and D, great, if not, that's okay."

D smirked. "So, M…o…u…s…e, what's the game plan?"

"I say we get some toys, some lube, and you call a friend that Barbie will enjoy and we can have a party at your place,"

Niiema said.

"I can hook that up," D said, pulling his phone from his pocket. He pressed the green call button and waited. "Marcus, you got Coke Can with you?"

D nodded. "Yeah, cool. I have a lady who needs some big dicks. Can y'all swing by around six tonight?" D smiled. "Yeah, that will be exactly what my little sex puppet needs. The more the better."

Barbie licked her lips and chewed on one of her nails. D hung up. "What did he say?" Barbie asked.

"My guy Marcus and Coke Can will be over in a few hours. We should get back to my place so we can tidy up."

Six in the evening rolled around. Niiema slept in D's arms in the bed nestled tight. He kissed her shoulder. "Mouse, it's time to get up."

Niiema yawned and blinked. "Is it that time already?"

D chuckled and kissed her shoulder again, his tongue lingering on the center. "We can leave my boys with Barbie and go to a hotel to get some quiet time. We don't have to have sex every night. I would like to get to know you better any way."

Niiema sighed and nuzzled against his shoulder. "Me too, but I haven't actually had sex with you yet. Let's stick to the plan, then we can move on to some new things tomorrow. I like this newer version of me. I'm not as mousey as you think I am."

D raised his hands in surrender. "Whatever you say."

Barbie stuck her head through the door with a frown and

said, "When you love birds are done, there's a knock at the door."

D got out of bed with a grumble. "Fucking Barbie, worthless whore… I just wanted to cuddle," he muttered, striding from the room.

Niiema tried to hold her smile but couldn't. He really did want out of the game and to settle down. The previous night wouldn't have shown that, but she saw how he looked at her, and she noticed more by the hour that all he wanted was Barbie out of his house. She hurried out behind him and stood next to Barbie, who was licking her lips.

"I never knew you were this slutty," Niiema whispered.

Barbie chuckled. "Where did you think I went between classes over the last semester." She cut her eyes at Niiema. "I was fucking the dean."

Niiema gasped. "What the fuck?"

Barbie chuckled. "It wasn't my first time kissing a girl either, by the way. I played innocent to make you comfortable."

"But why the deception?"

Barbie shrugged. "I didn't know if we would still be friends when you found out how I really am." She cleared her throat for the briefest instant. "I'm a slut, Niiema. That's who I am and don't want to change."

Niiema gasped when she heard what she said. "Why would I care if you're a slut?"

"Cause you're the quiet girl. Quiet girls don't hang with sluts."

Niiema's eyes hardened and she turned to look at her. She snatched her by the hair and kissed her passionately, rubbing her pussy. She leaned back and said, "You're right, I am quiet, but when you hear me scream tonight, know that quiet girls can fuck like sluts, but we don't cause we don't need too."

Barbie stood dumbfounded.

"Now, go get the dicks you want. I'm going to fuck D harder than any bitch walking the earth ever has."

Without another word, Niiema strode to the bedroom as the guests stepped through the threshold. Barbie's eyes opened wide when she saw two men walk in. She fluffed her hair and pressed her breasts up in her lingerie. She never even bothered to change back into clothes after her shower, they would just get in the way. One of the toys she took from the shop was a large butt plug that she had used for the last several hours.

D gave a pound to each man as they walked in. After he closed the door, he saw Barbie's hungry eyes search each man as they stood shoulder to shoulder. One was as tall as D but with a larger barreled chest, and the other man was as tall as she was.

"Fellas, this is Barbie, the chick I told you about."

They gave her a nod with a smile. The smaller man fished a joint out of his pocket and lit it. "So, you're the freak Barbie I've been hearing about at the club."

Then it hit her, she had seen him before. He was always quiet and shot pool near the door when she walked in. He never said a word, but his eyes stared through her every time she walked in. Barbie slowly nodded. "And you are?"

"Name's Coke Can, I run the block down there."

"You're Coke Can?"

He gave a wide smile. "That I am. And I hear you like party drugs. It just so happens I have a few of the best ones around."

He pulled two bags from his pocket and handed them to D. She licked her red lips and watched as D came over to the coffee table and dropped the bags in disgust. "Alright, I came through for you. This is where you get your ass fucked like you want."

Barbie twirled her hair around her finger and bit her lip. D shook his head with a sigh as Coke Can and Marcus walked into the living room. As they reached her, Niiema walked out and ran into D. He glanced down and smiled. "Mouse."

She grinned, staring up at him. "You can call me Mouse, I'm okay with that, but after tonight, you may say it in a different way."

D raised an eyebrow as Niiema opened her robe. She stood as tall as she could, then slipped out of it. She wore a tight see-through bra, accentuating her dark nipples. A pair of red see-through thong panties, and her pixies were wrapped on top of her head. Her dark skin glistened from lotion and the perfume she wore was so sweet that D inhaled deeply with a loud sigh.

Behind D, he heard Marcus say, "Goddamn, who the fuck is that?"

D turned slowly. "Fuck the white chick."

Marcus laughed. "You always had a thing for black chicks. Alright man, our dicks won't get anywhere near her holes, but if she grips one, it is what it is."

Niiema licked her lips and waved for D to come closer. She whispered in his ear. "If I take any dick tonight, it won't change how much I like you. You okay with that? I kinda like being a freak."

A smile crossed D's lips. He kissed her on the nose. "Mouse, if you want to fuck another dude, I won't say I'm good with it, but I'm not the exclusive type. You want to stretch your limits, feel free. No judgment."

Niiema leaped into his arms and he gripped her ass cheeks. They kissed for a moment. He set her down gently and turned around. With a shrug, he said, "Okay, change of plans. You two wanna dip your wick, she's good."

Barbie's eyes narrowed. "I thought this was my pair of dicks," she hissed.

Coke Can chuckled. "Yo shorty, chill out. Doubt you can take these both all night. We'll keep you entertained, but if the quiet chick wants an extra piece, let her get it."

Barbie pouted and glared at Niiema, who shrugged. "Told you not to mess with the quiet girl." She pointed at Marcus. "Not sure why you're still dressed, or the short one either." She heard D groan from behind her. He leaned down. "Easy with Coke Can, he's the head of The G Squad."

Niiema gasped. "Oh shit, I'm so sorry."

Coke Can smirked. "It's all good, shorty. You know why they call me Coke Can?"

Barbie directed his attention away from Niiema. "I don't give a fuck what she thinks, but I want to find out though." She dropped to her knees and snatched his belt buckle. Marcus unzipped his fly and stood next to her. Coke Can stared down at Barbie. "Yo, be careful, gir—"

Barbie gasped as he dropped his pants. Staring back at her was the thickest dick she had ever seen. It was wider than her upper forearm. She grinned and snatched it with two hands and licked the tip. "Soooo, that's why?" She sucked the tip with a pop. "This is gonna feel great in my ass."

Coke Can laughed. "Shorty, you're nuts."

She snatched Marcus in a death grip. "Yoooo."

"Get me some coke and heroin. I want to be so high I never come down," Barbie snapped.

Coke Can smirked and walked to the table and laid out several lines for her. Niiema walked over to Barbie. "What are you doing?"

"Getting high, Mouse. Thought that was obvious."

"You sure that you know what you're doing?" Niiema asked with a raised brow.

"Go fuck your boyfriend and let me do me."

Niiema shook her head. "Fine."

Niiema walked back over to D and leaned against his chest, taking a deep breath. She glanced up at his face, his eyes soft and caring. He kissed her on the forehead. "You good?"

Niiema gave a giddy smile and nodded as she lifted his tight polo shirt. She licked his nipple with the tip of her tongue. He massaged her ass cheeks. She moaned and drew a line down his abs with her tongue, their skin tones a wonderful contrast.

She continued to his belt loop and slowly undid the buckle and unzipped his pants. She lowered herself to her knees. She heard moaning behind her and glanced over her shoulder. Both Coke Can and Marcus held Barbie vertically as Marcus ate her out, her nose covered in white powder.

Niiema heard a lighter spark a blunt to life above her as she gripped D's boxer shorts and yanked them down. His huge erection popped free and almost smacked her in the face. She moved out of the way as it jettisoned past her. She giggled and snatched it. She heard Barbie groaning behind her and the blows to her ass cheeks.

"You like that shit huh, bitch?" She heard Coke Can say. Barbie groaned in response.

Niiema spun D around with his back facing Marcus and watched her friend get eaten out. She stared at them fondling Barbie's breasts as she took D's large cock in her mouth. She swallowed the head, having secretly rubbed oral gel around her jaw muscles. D groaned above her and held her head.

Coke Can kept glancing over at them and would wink and smile. Niiema winked back and knew he would be inside her one way or another before the night was out. She opened her mouth wide as she pushed D further in. She withdrew and spat on it, rubbing it along the shaft.

"Don't go easy on me tonight, D. We got plenty of time for that. Tonight, I want you balls deep inside me. Hard," she said from underneath him before licking the underside of his cock from balls to tip several times.

D leaned his head back as she stroked him. She stared Coke Can right in the eyes and flicked D's tip with her tongue. Coke Can blew her a kiss before spanking Barbie's ass again. Marcus shoved Barbie's mouth down to his balls and held her there. She choked and gripped his ass, her fingers dancing near his asshole. She spread his cheeks apart and flicked her index finger against it, eliciting a deep growl.

"Careful, bitch," Marcus hissed, tapping the top of her head.

She withdrew and gasped, wiping the spit from her chin.

"Bring that coke over here," Barbie demanded.

Marcus slid the mirror in front of her face and she waited. Glancing over her shoulder, she gave a nod to Coke Can. "Before I do this line, I want you to enter me balls deep, no lube. Ram it the fuck in."

"You really are a hoe," Coke Can said, sliding up behind her.

He pressed the tip to her opening and flicked it. She gave a loud groan and widened her stance. Lowering her face to the mirror, she closed one nostril and snorted the line as Coke Can entered her with a deep thrust. Her walls parted. She screamed, gripping Marcus' cock in a death grip. It stopped Niiema in her tracks.

"Fuck that pussy!" Barbie roared, swirling her hair around.

"What the fuck," D muttered in disgust.

Coke Can glanced at him with a shrug. "What, dog? This bitch is crazy."

Barbie leaned her head back to the coke lines, snorted, and shouted, "Fuck my face and pussy, now!"

Marcus dropped the mirror, snatched her hair, and shoved all nine inches down her throat as Coke Can slammed into her balls deep.

Niiema stood and smiled at D. "I like you, D. If you're gonna get mad, I won't participate, but I-----"

He touched her lips with his index finger. "Have fun. I'll let it slide this once, but after tonight ain't nobody else's dick going in my woman's pussy. Got me?"

"Oh, I'm you're woman now?"

D kissed her passionately and rubbed her cheeks. "Yes, you are."

Coke Can glanced over from a gagging sputtering mess that was Barbie and winked. "Hey, shorty. You wanna come lick this dick and get these juices off?"

Niiema sauntered over to him, sliding her index finger into the top of her panties. She held D's hand as she approached. With a smirk, she knelt in front of Coke Can and rubbed his chest. "This is a one-time favor from D. Punish this pussy."

"Say no more," Coke Can said, sliding out of Barbie.

Barbie glanced over her shoulder. "Why are you taking mine if you got your own?" she spat, the venom dripping from her tongue.

Niiema shook her head. "Marcus, shut her ass up and D, plug that ass."

D glared at Barbie, who licked her lips. "What's the matter, prett----"

D snatched her by the throat and lifted her to her knees. He pointed a finger in her face. "Look, you crazy bitch, I'm only doing this because Niiema wants to have fun." He slapped her and spun her back to Marcus, who slammed his dick back in her mouth.

D spat on his hand, yanked her butt plug out, and gave one last glance to Niiema. "Good luck with that monster, Mouse."

She blew him a kiss.

Chapter 8

Niiema widened her jaw as Coke Can slid the tip in her mouth. It was so wide that her cheeks bulged. She gave a loud sigh as she glanced up into his eyes. She took one of his hands and placed it on her head. Coke Can took the signal and bobbed her head up and down on his shaft.

D slapped Barbie on the ass and she arched her back high in the air, leaving a large hand print on her pink flesh. She twerked her ass cheeks as he got behind her. Marcus shoved his dick further down her throat as she heaved and spat. D gripped her by the back of the head and gave a strong push.

Barbie dry heaved and lifted up. D caught her under the stomach and rammed his dick into her ass. Barbie slammed back, withdrew Marcus from her mouth, and screeched. "Fuuuuu-" Marcus snatched her hair from D and shoved his dick so far down her throat that he stutter stepped.

Niiema watched the spectacle unfold and inched more of

Coke Can into her mouth. She gagged, withdrew, spat, and bobbed again. She could hear Coke Can grunting as the tip hit the back of her tonsils. She took one final shove and got half way down the shaft.

"Yo shorty, that tongue is magical," he sighed.

Niiema pressed her tongue against the bottom of his cock, withdrew it, and pushed him back on his ass. Before he could recover, she climbed over him like a spider and mounted above him, her juices running down her leg. D turned and slid a hand over Niiema's breast and pinched her nipple. Niiema kissed his hand and then rubbed her clit as she touched the tip of Coke Can's dick.

Niiema let the tip rest at her opening as D turned back around and slammed into Barbie with long strokes. Barbie screamed as he plowed deep in her. She withdrew from Marcus's cock and croaked. "Bring me the coke and H."

Marcus shook his head and put a line of each on the mirror. She glanced up at Marcus. "Time for a DP."

She slid back on D's pole and groaned, shuddering as she had an orgasm. Marcus moved under her and slid his cock into her. She bellowed. "Oh, fuck. That's---" Her lip curled. "The spot."

D heard Niiema whimper behind him as she slowly slid down onto Coke Can's shaft. Niiema winced again then slid a little further. "Yo, hold up, shorty." Coke Can reached over to the table and poured some of the lube on his dick.

Niiema rubbed some on her clit and then slid a little further. She glanced at D, who was plowing into Barbie. Barbie bucked and squirmed, screaming in ecstasy, then moved her head to the mirror and hoovered up both lines before arching her back. D and Marcus went with her.

Barbie's whole body shook as the drugs and penetration drove her over the edge. She snorted loudly as Marcus pounded up from the bottom and D held her hips. Both holes plugged, Barbie gripped Marcus's pecks and shuddered a third time, then sprang up, squirting all over his chest while she rubbed her clit.

Barbie collapsed into D, who caught her. She trembled for a few moments, then hopped on Marcus and he slammed it back in. Barbie rubbed her nose and continued to ride him. She waved D over as she came again from Marcus's blows.

Niiema watched as everything unfolded. She slid a little further down Coke Can's shaft and stopped. "You okay, shorty?"

Niiema stood up and nodded. "I just don't feel right doing this. I only want to be with D."

D heard his name and pulled out immediately. "What the fuck?" Barbie shouted.

"Yo, I'm about to nut," Marcus shouted.

Coke Can gave a head nod at Niiema. "Ain't no shame in that, shorty. Let me go deal with that crazy hoe. Y'all have fun."

D slid past him and took Niiema in his arms, kissing her passionately. He tucked his cock between his legs and whispered, "I'll be right back."

Niiema gave one last glance at Barbie, who was being pounded into submission. She watched Marcus ejaculate down Barbie's throat as Coke Can continued to shove himself further inside her. Barbie screamed and landed face down as Coke Can plowed away.

"Here you go, crazy bitch," Coke Can roared as he came deep inside her ass. Barbie grunted as she came one final time and fell to the floor, drenched. Marcus and Coke Can shook their heads. "I think she's done, yo."

Coke Can pulled his pants up. "Yo, Mouse. Tell D we said thanks and to get rid of this crazy bitch as soon as possible. We out."

Niiema smiled and waved. "Bye fellas."

Niiema strolled into the bedroom and closed the door. She heard D cursing out loud as he washed his dick off. All she could hear was, "I just wanted to be with Niiema, but *no*, crazy hoe had to fuck that all up."

He paused as he heard a giggle behind him. "You okay over there, D?"

D mumbled something else and strode across the room, sweeping her off her feet. He kissed her neck passionately and held her tight. With both arms extended, he gently lowered her to the mattress, making sure her head rested on the satin pillow. She purred and rubbed her soft spot.

D lay beside her, nose to nose. "Mouse, I-----"

Niiema placed her index finger on his lips. "Just because I didn't want to take another man's dick doesn't mean that I don't want to take yours. We can be gushy tonight when we watch a movie on Netflix, but right now, I want that Big D."

D smirked and let her lay him back on the bed. She traced her index finger along his stomach down to his naval, flicking her tongue against his nipple. Niiema slid her hand over his dick and then kissed her way down to his belly button. Gripping him in her hand, she lowered her face down, flicking her tongue on the tip, staring into his soft blue eyes.

Niiema widened her jaw and took him in her mouth. She started slow at first, then started working both hands along the shaft. Her head bobbed up and down as she began to moisten. D slid his long arm over her ass and pressed his index finger against her slit. She moaned and wiggled up against it.

D slid his finger inside the warmth, aiming it up. Niiema gasped and sighed as she started to get a little wilder. Slamming his dick down her throat, her whole body convulsed. Yanking his balls, Niiema tugged until she heard him groan. She sprang up and hovered over the shaft, teasing her opening with a loud moan.

Niiema leaned her head next to D's. "Are you ready for this hot pussy?" she breathed into his ear.

"Hell yeah. Can I eat you out first so you're ready for it?"

"Nah, I'm ready. Get me that rabbit over there so I can have a little more umph."

D snatched it off the table and handed it to her. Before sliding back down his chest, she kissed his nose and licked his lips. D gave a wide grin. "God, had I known quiet chicks were so hot in the room, I would have been fucking them a long time ago."

"That's what happens when you mess with the hoes who have to flaunt their shit cause they don't spend time in the library. The brain is sexier than a pair of tits," she cooed, sliding onto his dick.

She turned the rabbit on and the humming cracked the still air. She hovered over D and pressed the rabbit to her clit, eliciting a deep groan from her. Niiema snatched his dick and slid the tip into her wet pussy. D stifled a groan as the head pressed through her opening. Niiema winced.

"You okay, Mouse."

"I'm fine, baby, just my first time with a massive dick. I'll be okay in a minute."

D leaned forward without shifting her position and kissed her arms as she slid him further in. He stared into her eyes as she worked her way down the shaft. A soft whimper escaped her lips as she bit her bottom lip. D held her hips, gently helping her wiggle down on it at her own pace.

It seemed like an eternity before she made it halfway. The buzzing of the vibrator drove her clit into hyper drive. She glanced over her shoulder, expecting Barbie to burst in at any moment to ruin her pleasure. D moved her face back to him.

"Don't worry about that hoe. I just hope she doesn't steal my shit."

Niiema laughed as she slid further down. "Can I help you with the vibrator?" D asked.

Niiema nodded and let him take it. He licked it and groaned. "God, that's sweet."

She blushed until he placed it back on her clit. She rubbed her dark breasts, then ran her fingers through her pixies. She slid a little further down, her juices starting to lather his dick. The rest of the shaft slid in without a problem, until the last inch, which couldn't bottom out in her.

"Holy fuck, that's huge. I feel it in my g----" She bucked so hard that she slid several inches up the shaft. D lowered her back down gently. Niiema bit her bottom lip and screamed. She heard Barbie wake up and shout, "Keep it down, bitch. You cocked blocked."

"Fuck off," D shouted. "And get the fuck out of my place."

They heard something crash against the wall. D readied to get out of bed, but Niiema, focused on him, pressed her hands around his cheeks. "Baby, it's okay, just keep inside me. It feels so good." She bucked again and her eyes rolled back. She shivered from her tailbone to her neck.

D slowly started moving her back and forth on his lap as more items crashed around the apartment. His concentration broke again. "Niiema, she's breaking all my shit," he spat.

Niiema's eyes turned cold and she hopped off and stormed toward the door. She flung it open and a naked, messy Barbie stood there looking wild as she spat on the floor. Niiema stepped into the living room.

"So, I guess this means our friendship is over?" Niiema hissed.

"Goddamn right, quiet bitch," Barbie shouted, throwing a vase against the wall.

"Barbie, look, I want you to leave." She tossed her the clothes. "Please."

Barbie glared at her, then threw her clothes on. She snatched the drugs off the table and shoved them in her purse. "This isn't over, bitch." She rose up onto her tippy toes and shouted over Niiema's shoulder. "And D, just to let you know, I'm *not* on the pill. And when I have your kid, I'm taking everything you got. Because you're a deadbeat drug dealer!"

"You motherfucking whore," D roared, scrambling out of bed.

Niiema blocked the door as D stood fuming behind her. "Babe, please move."

"Barbie, leave right now. I won't let him past me. But don't make me come over there and whoop your ass," Niiema said, her voice like steel.

"You wouldn't dare."

Niiema took a step forward, but D held her tight. "Barbie, I think this is over. So, leave or I will call Coke Can and have him escort you out, then leave you naked on the block. All kinds of mean wolves out there that will take a bite right outta your hoe ass."

Barbie stood still for a moment, clenching her fists. Finally, a single tear dropped from her eye. "Fuck both of you. I thought we were friends, Niiema."

"We were, but you are a psychopath." Niiema pointed at the front door. "Now leave."

Barbie threw another glass nearby above their heads, sending shards of glass over them and sprinted for the door. Niiema felt D tense and take a step forward. She held him back. "Let her go, D. It's not worth getting arrested."

The front door slammed and then it was quiet. Niiema shook her head. "I always heard rumors of how she was, but I never wanted to believe it."

"You knew she was like this?" D asked, the anger evident in his voice.

Niiema turned and glanced up at him. "I always give people the benefit of the doubt, D. You're a drug dealer for the time being, but it doesn't bother me because I know you're a good person. After all this drama, I'm glad I found a positive energy and lost a negative one."

D shook his head. "And now I'm fucked because she could be pregnant."

Niiema smirked. "Well, she is a compulsive liar and I know for a fact she takes her pill."

"And how do you know?"

"She lied about everything she ever said. She just started her period yesterday. I'm sure you didn't notice the ring around your dick." She chuckled. "We'll be okay." She grabbed D's hand and led him back into the bedroom. "Now, if you don't mind, I'd like to get fucked and then take a long nap with you before the end of the night."

"Are you sure I can't be romantic?" he asked as she crawled on the bed, her naked ass lifted high. She lay face down on the bed and moaned. She slapped her ass as she slid her fingers to her clit.

Without waiting for her permission, D swiftly clamped his mouth around her pussy from behind and parted her ass cheeks. He licked from her clit to her asshole. D tongued it for a minute as Niiema's groans and moans increased.

Niiema grabbed his head and pressed him in harder between her cheeks. D moaned and slid his hand around her legs to her clit, rubbing it with her. She pressed back on him, sliding her hands to her ass cheeks. D moved faster on her clit, rolling it in a counter clockwise motion.

Niiema gasped and moaned. "D, I----"

"Me too," he murmured as he blew hot air against her mound. He rolled his head under her legs and started sucking her pussy lips. Niiema lowered onto his face with a giggle and gripped her fingers tight to his scalp, massaging it.

She started riding back and forth and screamed as she orgasmed, her legs tightening around his face. She rubbed her breasts and bucked several times. D lifted her by the ass cheeks and said, "Keep cumming, it's sweater than pineapple." Then he lowered her back down.

Niiema spun on his face, which she had never done before, and leaned over. She snatched his dick and stretched her jaw muscles. She sucked the head as D squirmed under her. He clenched her ass cheeks further, tightening his grip.

"Ready, D?" Niiema murmured, gently running her fingernails down his shaft. She took a deep breath and swallowed seven inches. She gave a loud gag and D knew what she wanted. He reached around and pressed her head as softly as he could, but Niiema threw a hand over his and pushed harder.

D got the hint and pressed down, thrusting his pelvis up, driving another three inches into the back of her throat. She gagged again and D held her tight, knowing that's what she liked. As Niiema sucked more in, he slid his tongue deep inside her pussy and licked as far forward as he could, searching for her G spot.

Niiema bucked several times from gagging and cumming at the same time. She withdrew from his dick with a final gag and spat on the shaft. Niiema rubbed the spit over her breast and then slid forward off D's face, who groaned in protest. "Niiema, please," he whispered.

"D, I want to ride this donkey and then we can do whatever you want tonight. I'm all yours for as long as you'll have me. So, no need for the soft stuff right now. We can spoon later and make out as long as you want. And if you want to eat me till I pass out, that's awesome too." She let out a soft groan as she slid the head of his dick over her opening.

"Whatever you say, Mouse," D said quietly, resting his palms around her hour glass waist.

Niiema smiled and slid him inside her and this time it went in easier. She slid to his balls with a squeal. "Fuck, that's big. I could get used to this."

"You can have it all, Mouse."

Niiema slowly slid back against his pelvis and he groaned, her tight walls enveloping him. He pushed up slightly, bottoming the rest inside her. She grunted in approval and bit her lip. Niiema's eyes flung open and she screamed. A feeling exploded inside of her that she had never in her life experienced.

As seasoned as D was, he knew the sign of an oncoming squirt. He slid her off his dick with one hand, while rubbing her clit furiously with the other.

Niiema gasped. "What----"

A few droplets of fluid dripped from her, then a long stream came out, sending a tremendous euphoric feeling similar to the ecstasy she orgasmed on. She pitched forward as she felt spasms in her legs, and her eyes rolled into the back of her head. She gasped and hissed, her whole body convulsing. D held her close to his chest as the remains of her squirt rolled down it, soaking the sheets underneath them. Niiema reared back with a scream so loud D couldn't help but grin.

Niiema's eyes crossed and she took haggard breaths. D didn't wait to explain why her juices were flowing out of control. That would come later. He lifted her up and held her over his shaft. "Okay, Mouse. No more Mr. Nice Guy."

D slammed her down on his shaft. She screamed and rubbed her body all over, her hips gyrating across his lap. He snatched her pixies and yanked her head back as he drove himself up into her, lifting the pair of them off the bed. Niiema started riding back and forth until D lowered them back down. He started slamming up so fast that Niiema's screams echoed in the room. She gasped and yelled, "Oh my GOD, Deeeeeeeeee!"

Her body convulsed and her eyes rolled as they always did. Her lips turned into a sneer. D's balls slapped the bottom of her pussy as she threw her ass down. In one motion, D had her on her knees and slapped her ass. He pumped so hard it drove her forward.

"You can tap out anytime, Mouse," he shouted, arching his back.

Niiema slammed back into him and screamed, "Not even close."

D yanked her pixies back again and wrapped them around one hand, slamming into her harder than before.

"That's it, Daddy," she screamed, rubbing her clit furiously. "That feelings coming back."

"You're squirting," D moaned.

He yanked his dick out and thrust his hand over her pelvis, pressing down as hard as he could as his four fingers slammed into her. He withdrew them in a flourish and she squirted again. She found that if she pinched her nipples as hard as she could, the feeling intensified. She fell forward and D leaned over and slid back inside her.

He placed his palms in front of her shoulders, locking her in. He leaned back and slammed so hard her hair dropped over the edge of the bed. "Cum on me, Daddy," she screamed.

D could feel the pressure in his balls mounting. He held on as long as he could. One stroke…another stroke…and one last stroke. He pulled out and Niiema spun around underneath him. He sprayed his cum over her breasts with a tremendous growl, his left eyelid twitching. Niiema rubbed the semen all over her body. D yanked his shaft so furiously that the ejaculate kept dripping from his tip. Niiema leaned forward and swallowed the tip. She glanced up, withdrew for a moment, and shouted. "Push that nut out with everything you got. I'll help you."

D's dick was on fire as he shook. He pressed his lower back muscles as hard as he could, unsure whether piss would come out. He prayed it wouldn't as he gently touched Niiema's temples, massaging them. She slammed a finger up his ass and pressed against his prostate as hard as she could.

D shot another load that hurt so much he hissed. "Owwwwwww."

Niiema yanked on his dick, spat on it to lube it up, and kept it up until D began to retreat. She slid her finger out and yanked his ass cheeks forward. With one final push, the rest drained. His balls and kidneys ached.

Niiema swallowed everything and with a relish, she licked his fire red tip. He winced and lay back. Niiema smirked. "And that's why you never mess with a quiet chick. What's my name?"

D cringed and whimpered, "Mouse."